The Best Place

SUSAN MEDDAUGH

HOUGHTON MIFFLIN COMPANY BOSTON 1999

Walter Lorraine Books

For Trauts

Walter Lorraine (wl) Books

Copyright © 1999 by Susan Meddaugh

All rights reserved. For information about permission
to reproduce selections from this book, write to Permissions,
Houghton Mifflin Company, 215 Park Avenue South,
New York, New York 10003.

Library of Congress Cataloging-in-Publication Data

Meddaugh, Susan.
   The best place / Susan Meddaugh.
      p.   cm.
   Summary: After traveling around the world to make sure that the
view from his screen porch is the best, an old wolf tries drastic
measures to get his house back from the rabbit family that had
bought it.
   ISBN 0-395-97994-3
   [1. Wolves—Fiction. 2. Animals—Fiction.   3. Views—Fiction.
4. Behavior—Fiction.] I. Title.
PZ7.M51273Bf   1999
[E]—DC21   98-50184
                                             CIP
                                             AC

Printed in the United States of America

WOZ 10 9 8 7 6 5 4 3 2 1

An old wolf and a bird were watching the sun set
from the wolf's screen porch.
"Nice view," said the bird.
"I'll say!" the wolf agreed.

"This screen porch is magical," said the wolf. "Where else
can you be inside and outside at the same time? I think
my screen porch is the best place in the whole world!"
But the bird, who had traveled a bit, said, "How do
you know? You've never been anyplace else."

That night the old wolf had trouble sleeping. How *did* he know? Maybe there was a better view, a place more magical than his own screen porch. He decided to find out before he became an even older wolf.

The next day he put his house up for sale, and
a week later he sold it to a nice young couple.
"I hope you enjoy the screen porch as much as I have,"
he told them.
He waved good-bye to all his neighbors and set off to see
the world.

The wolf's travels took him to many interesting places.
He floated down the Orinoco with a native guide.
He couldn't help remembering how the mosquitoes *never*
got to him on his old screen porch.

He was awed by the desert.
"That's a lot of sand," he said.
But it was too hot.
"There was always a nice breeze on my screen porch,"
he thought.

He got soaked seeing the sights in London.
"I know a place where you can be outside when it's raining and never get wet," he told the umbrella salesman.
"Is that good?" asked the duck.

Finally the wolf's journey brought him home.
"I'll just see how those rabbits are doing," he thought.
When he saw his old house with its wonderful screen
porch, he was overcome with longing.
"Why did I ever sell my house?" he thought. "I must get
it back!"

So he said, "You rabbits should really get out and see the world. You'll never know what you're missing."

"Travel with this crowd?" the rabbit said with a laugh, and he marched all his children inside for dinner.

The wolf knocked on the door.
"Please," he said. "I want to
buy my house back."
"It's not for sale," said the
rabbits, and they shut
the door.

The wolf went to the window.
"*Pul-leeze!*" he whined. "I'll pay you double!"
"No," said the rabbits, and they closed the curtains.

The old wolf was upset.

"I'm not leaving until I get my house back," he shouted.

He started to jump up and down.

"MY HOUSE! MY HOUSE! GIMME! GIMME! GIMME!"

he yelled. "I WANT MY HOUSE AND I WANT IT NOW!"

The rabbits locked the door.

"Owooo!" howled the wolf.

He howled and growled, and the ground shook beneath his feet. And although the wolf had lived peacefully for years with his neighbors, now they noticed how *big* he was, how *sharp* his teeth were.

At last the wolf fell silent. There was silence in the forest as well.

"Oh dear," thought the wolf. "That was quite a temper tantrum."

Completely embarrassed, he hurried away down the path.

"I've been a bad, bad wolf," he said as he sat by himself
in another part of the forest. "I guess I'll never get
my house back now."
And he thought, "I must apologize to those rabbits."

But a simple apology didn't seem enough.
"I know," said the wolf. "I'll make them a special dinner.
It will be a feast fit for a rabbit."

He chopped and stirred and cooked and tasted until he
had a table full of delicious vegetarian treats. Then off
he went to invite the rabbit family for dinner.

The rabbits saw the wolf running up the path.
"DINNER IS SERVED!" he shouted. "DINNER IS SERVED!"

They saw the napkin around his neck and the fork and spoon
in his hands.

"Help!" cried the rabbits. "The wolf wants to eat us for dinner!"

Their neighbors, fearing the worst, came running to the rescue. Before the wolf could explain, they chased him into the forest.

"GO AWAY!" they shouted. "AND DON'T COME BACK!"

It wasn't until a passing bird spotted the wolf's beautiful
banquet that they realized a mistake had been made.
"We have misjudged the wolf," said Mrs. Rabbit.
But it was too late to set things straight. The old wolf,
confused and frightened, had run deep into the forest.

He ran until it was too dark to see where he was going.
Then he climbed a tree and fell asleep.

The next morning the old wolf woke up to a sight more
beautiful than anything he had seen in all of his travels,
more beautiful even than the view from his old
screen porch.

The wolf knew what he had to do.
First he wrote a sincere letter of apology to
the Rabbit family. He hoped that everyone
would someday forgive him for his terrible
tantrum.

Then the wolf started to build a new home.

It was hard and lonely work. He was wondering if he would ever be able to finish the job, when out of the forest, one after another, came all of his old neighbors.

"Can we help?" they asked.

"You bet!" said the wolf.

Soon a magnificent structure began to grow at the top of the tallest tree.

"I think I've finally found the best place in the world,"
said the wolf.
"Yes," the bird agreed. "It is a beautiful view."
But the wolf said, "That's not what makes it best."